For my mum – R.K.
For Lollipop and Silly Nose – W.A.

First published in Great Britain in 2006 and in the USA in 2007 by
Frances Lincoln Children's Books, 4 Torriano Mews, Torriano Avenue, London NW5 2RZ
www.franceslincoln.com

Distributed in the USA by Publishers Group West

British Library Cataloguing in Publication Data
available on request

ISBN 10: 1-84507-481-5
ISBN 13: 978-1-84507-481-4

Illustrated with pencil, coloured crayons, watercolours and inks
Set in Usherwood and Merlin

Printed in China
1 3 5 7 9 8 6 4 2

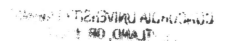

The Secret World of
MAGIC

Rosalind Kerven

Illustrated by
Wayne Anderson

F

FRANCES LINCOLN
CHILDREN'S BOOKS

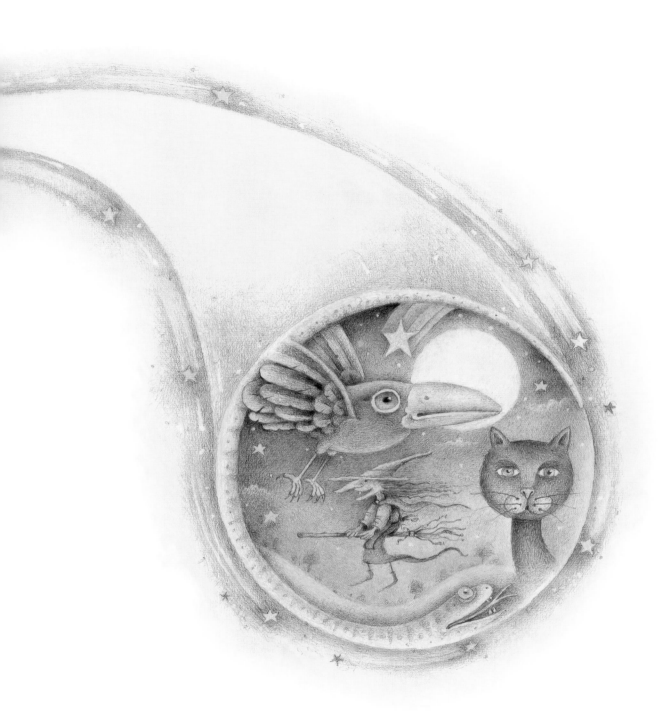

Contents

DO YOU BELIEVE IN MAGIC?

Imagine: you are standing in the shadows of your strangest dreams.

Here impossible things happen every day. Birds turn into beautiful women. Horses sprout wings and fly. Wishes come true. Precious jewels fall from the sky. Ladders lead up through the clouds to secret worlds. People and things vanish.

This is magic. Believe in it! Marvel at it! Let it seep under your skin and give you the shivers…

Magic is dark and mysterious, wide as the world, older than fairy tales. Its secrets lie hidden in ancient, dusty books and storytellers' memories. But its powers are not dead – they are only sleeping. If only you can learn the right chants, songs and spells – you may even bring them to life!

Is this true? Does magic really work?

Well, explore the ideas in this book. Some are lost in the mists of time, but maybe others happened not so very long ago…

MAKERS OF MAGIC

Beware of weird creatures! Keep away from people in mysterious dark robes! They may try to impress you with their magic powers. They may tempt you with promises. But they are sure to be dangerous.

Luckily you are not likely to meet these magic-makers, for they hardly ever mix with ordinary people. They like to lie low in tumbledown houses, ruined castles, caves, deserts, earth-mounds and forests. They only come out at night.

Witches, Wizards, Enchanters and Sorcerers can be found on the prowl in every corner of the world. They are easy to recognise because they usually carry a magic wand or staff. They can fly, change shape and become invisible. They can also read the future, bring dead things back to life, brew love potions and cast all kinds of wicked spells.

Jinn (also known as Genies)

live in the legendary emerald mountains of Qaf. They are
usually invisible, but if ever you visit the Arabian deserts,
you may suddenly see one appear out of thin air.
Jinn can take any shape. Most are evil and often look
like beetles, toads or scorpions. But good Jinn
sometimes appear in the shapes of men or snakes.
They can grant wishes and carry people and
buildings right across the world in a flash.

Fairies

lurk in trees or old houses and dance under the moon
all over Britain, Ireland, Europe and the Americas.
Sometimes they snatch a baby away and leave
a changeling in its place. They can fly,
cast spells, grant wishes and turn
junk and rubbish into gold.

MAGIC CHILDREN

Are you the youngest in your family?
If so, you may have a gift for magic!
In fairy tales, when three brothers or sisters
set out on a quest, usually only the youngest
one is brave and clever enough to finish it.

A seventh child may have magic healing powers
and see into the future. A seventh son of a seventh
son, or a seventh daughter of a seventh
daughter is said to have
the greatest magic gifts
of all.

Twin brothers were once thought
to be very special. Stories tell of twins
going on dangerous journeys
and killing monsters.

STONE-RIBS

*Stone-Ribs was a Native American boy born
with magic in his soul! One day he caught
a big fish. He cut it up, put the skin over his
head – and turned himself into a fish!*

*Stone-Ribs was swimming in the sea when an evil
whale appeared. Everyone was terrified. But Stone-Ribs
swam up and killed it. Then he put on the dead whale's
skin – and turned into a whale!*

*An ugly sea-monster decided to take revenge on
Stone-Ribs. It trapped him in its lair – but the boy
changed back into his fish shape, slipped out of the door
and swam away.*

*And so Stone-Ribs went on changing shape from boy to fish
to whale and back again. In this way he destroyed many
more terrible sea-monsters. Everyone was very grateful.*

*In the end an eagle stole Stone-Ribs' magic skins, so he
couldn't change shape any more. But by that time
all the monsters had fled and everyone
was cheering Stone-Ribs as
a mighty hero!*

MAGIC SPELLS

Imagine performing impossible deeds!

Imagine enchanting someone! Imagine changing something completely!

Magic spells can do all this.

Four ways to cast a spell

★ Chant secret words in a mysterious language.

★ Collect spiders' webs, frog-spawn and other weird ingredients from forests
and wild places, then brew them up in a steaming cauldron.

★ Wear or wave a magic object – a cloak, cap, wand or staff.

★ Touch the object of your spell or blow on it gently.

A spell can...

★ Send someone
into a long, deep sleep.

★ Open a door in solid rock.

★ Carry someone across the world in a flash.

★ Make people
and things invisible.

RAINING JEWELS

*An old man living in India studied ancient magic books and learnt
an amazing spell. When the stars were shining in a particular pattern,
he would say some magic words. Then jewels would fall from the sky!*

*One day he went on a long journey, and was captured by bandits.
They refused to set him free unless he paid them a lot of money.
Unfortunately, the old man didn't have any money with him.
However, the stars were exactly right that night for working his spell,
so he softly muttered the magic words. At once rubies, emeralds
and diamonds came raining down!*

*The bandits went mad with excitement. "Make more!" they cried.
But the stars had moved. Although he tried hard, the old man couldn't
make the spell work again. The bandits were furious. They jumped
on the old man and killed him. Then they began to fight over the jewels,
until they had killed each other as well.*

*It would have been better for everyone if that
particular spell had never been discovered!*

SHAPE-CHANGING SPELLS

Sometimes wicked magicians
and witches take revenge
on their enemies by turning
their children into
animals or birds.

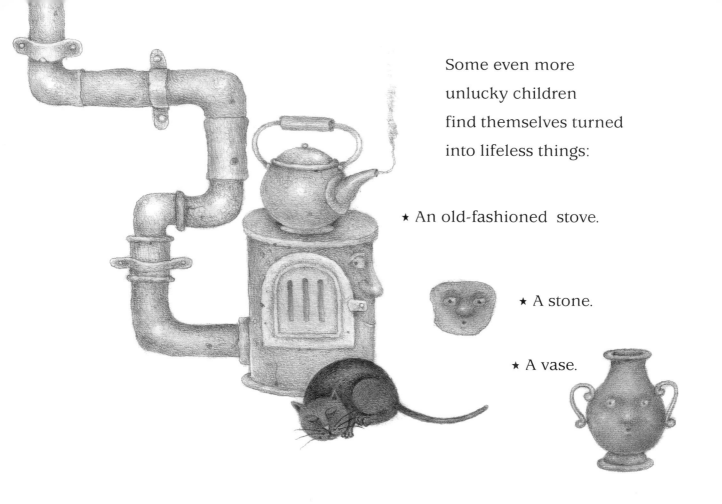

Some even more
unlucky children
find themselves turned
into lifeless things:

★ An old-fashioned stove.

★ A stone.

★ A vase.

How to save your friends from this horrible fate

Don't worry too much if this happens to one of your friends.
There are several easy ways to break these nasty spells:

★ Kiss the animal or thing that your friend has
turned into.

★ Keep totally silent for seven whole years.

★ Travel to the ends of the earth to find
your friend.

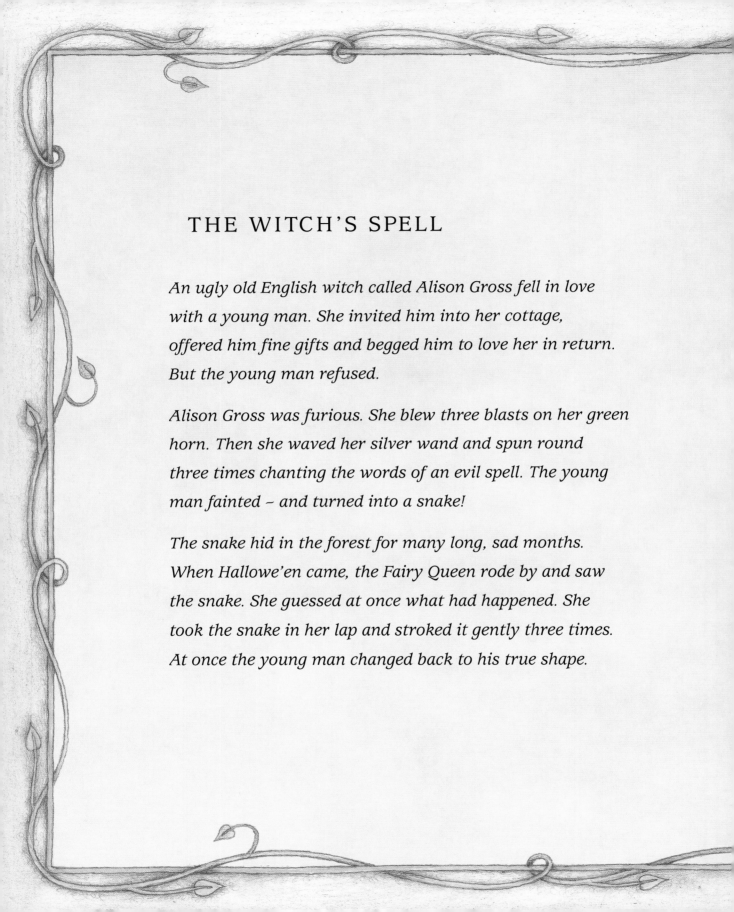

THE WITCH'S SPELL

An ugly old English witch called Alison Gross fell in love with a young man. She invited him into her cottage, offered him fine gifts and begged him to love her in return. But the young man refused.

Alison Gross was furious. She blew three blasts on her green horn. Then she waved her silver wand and spun round three times chanting the words of an evil spell. The young man fainted – and turned into a snake!

The snake hid in the forest for many long, sad months. When Hallowe'en came, the Fairy Queen rode by and saw the snake. She guessed at once what had happened. She took the snake in her lap and stroked it gently three times. At once the young man changed back to his true shape.

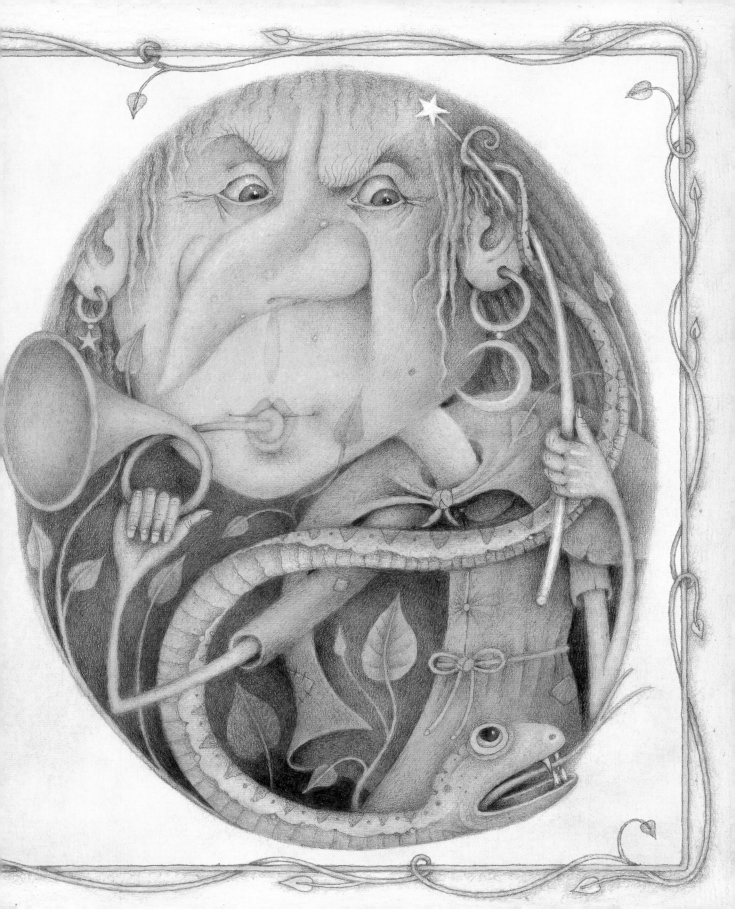

Some very special people can change their shapes whenever they want.

Swan Maidens are found all over the world. They look like swans when they fly in the sky. But when they go swimming, they take off their feather cloaks and turn into girls.

Dragon Kings and Princesses live in China, Japan and Korea. Sometimes they look like people. But if they swallow magic pearls, they turn into dragons.

Selkies live in the seas around Scotland, Ireland and Norway. They look like ordinary seals. But when they come out on dry land, they shed their skins and turn into beautiful women.

Tree Women

are found in parts of Africa. They are trees which can turn themselves into beautiful women. They often marry ordinary men. However, if anyone gives away their secret, they turn back into trees again.

Spider-Woman

(also known as Grandmother Spider) lives amongst the Native American people of the south-western USA. She is a very wise old lady, and often changes herself into a tiny grey spider. Then she runs up people's arms and whispers good advice in their ears.

WISHES

In fairy tales, wishes always used to come true.

★ Old wise women sometimes granted wishes as a reward to kind children who had helped them.

★ Fairies often gave three wishes to people they liked.

★ You could wish on a star, or over a magic ring (see page 32).

You could make a wish just by saying, "I wish I had…" and whatever you wanted would appear by magic. Nowadays wishing takes longer – but it can still work!

Wishing Wells

Castles, gardens and even
shopping centres sometimes have
a wishing well. If you see one, throw
a coin into the water, close your eyes
and make a wish!

Wish-Bones

If your family has a roast chicken for dinner, ask
for the wish-bone afterwards. Get someone to help
you pull it until it breaks in half. The person who
gets the bigger part can make a wish.

Be careful how you wish!

★ Keep your wish secret, or it won't come true.

★ Make it clear exactly what you are wishing for.

★ Don't wish for the wrong thing by mistake.

★ Don't wish for something selfish – it will lead to trouble.

★ Don't waste your wish – you won't get another one.

THE SAUSAGE WISH

Rose, Fergus and old Norah lived together in a tumbledown cottage in Ireland. They were always complaining, "Oh, we're so poor! Och, we're so hungry!"

Well, one day a cunning little fairy man appeared. "Quick!" he said. "I'll grant you a wish each. Who's going first?"

"Me," said Rose. "I wish I could have a juicy, fat sausage in my frying pan." At once the sausage appeared.

"What a stupid wish," sneered Fergus. "That sausage will be eaten in no time. I wish it would stick to the end of your silly nose!" At once, the sausage jumped out of the pan and on to Rose's nose.

"You bully!" screamed old Norah. "I wish the other end of the sausage would stick to your nose, Fergus!" And so it did. What a sight Rose and Fergus looked, jumping around, stuck together by a sausage!

"You've used up all your wishes, my friends," chuckled the fairy man. "You could have wished for wonderful treasures – but instead, you wasted everything!"

And with that, he vanished.

LUCKY CHARMS

 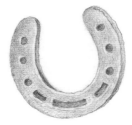

★ An old coin　　★ A horseshoe　　★ An unusual pebble...

could really be amulets or charms. These have magical powers to keep you safe and bring you luck.

Try carrying one around in your pocket or wear it on a string round your neck, and see what happens.

Four-leaf clovers are especially lucky. Some people say they help you spot fairies and see into the future.

Rainbows bring a special kind of luck.

Excalibur

King Arthur had a wonderful sword called Excalibur. The scabbard he kept it in was a powerful amulet. As long as he wore it at his side, nothing could kill him. The sword and the scabbard were made for him by fairy smiths in the mysterious Otherworld of Avalon (see page 43).

If you go to the rainbow's end, you will find a crock of gold waiting there for you.

BEWITCHED THINGS

Take great care with any object that you haven't used before!
It might have been bewitched. If so, it will behave very strangely.
Some bewitched objects are really useful – but others can
be dangerous.

Magic tables and tablecloths

If you say "Set yourself!", a bewitched table
or tablecloth will conjure up a delicious
spread of food and drink.

Philosopher's Stone

You could make a fortune if you find
a strange lump of rock like this.
It might have the power to turn
cheap metal into gold!

Bewitched musical instruments

If someone plays one of these,
everyone who hears it has to start dancing.
Sometimes even the furniture dances too!

No one can stop dancing until the musician stops
playing. But the musician can't stop playing until
the magic spell is removed. And if that doesn't
happen, the music and dancing will go on for ever!

Magic Rings

These can:

* ★ Protect you from danger.
* ★ Grant wishes.
* ★ Conjure up genies to obey your commands.
  * ★ Make a heap of gold grow bigger every day.

If you wear a magic ring all the time, you might end up ruling the world!

Some magic rings start to work as soon as you put them on your finger. With others, you need to rub them, or chant secret words over them.

Magic Cauldrons

You can find huge cooking pots like this in old houses in Wales and Ireland. People say that anyone brave enough to jump inside one will live for ever!

CERIDWEN'S CAULDRON

Ceridwen the Welsh witch once brewed up a magic soup in her wonderful Cauldron of Knowledge. She planned to give it to her son Afagddu to make him wise.

She called in a boy called Gwion. "Guard this cauldron for a year," she said, "but do not touch or taste the brew!"

For many months Gwion guarded the brew. One day it started to bubble and splash. Three drops fell on his hand and scalded him. He licked them off and swallowed them. At once he got all the wisdom that Ceridwen wanted her son to have!

Ceridwen was furious. She changed herself into a hen. Then she turned Gwion into a grain of corn and ate him. But nine months later he was born again, still full of the magic cauldron's wisdom. When he grew up, he changed his name to Taliesin and became a famous poet who could predict the future.

ENCHANTED TRAVEL

People who know magic never have to walk
anywhere! They can cross land and water
much faster than cars, ships and even planes.

Seven League Boots can carry you
right across the world in a single stride. If you ever
meet a giant, ask if you can borrow his.

Magic Carpets can whisk you away to exotic places.
King Solomon liked to put his throne on a special silk carpet.
The wind carried it across the sky
at his command.

Learn to Fly...

★ On a broomstick, like a witch.

★ On a magic beast like Pegasus,
the flying horse in Greek mythology
who carried monster-slaying heroes
on his back.

★ On a cloud trapeze,
like the mischievous Chinese
super-hero Monkey who tried to take over
the whole universe.

★ 35 ★

THE FLYING CAP

One day, a Scottish boy got lost in the forest. A kind bear showed him the way to a nearby cottage. There, two strange old ladies took him in and put him to bed.

At midnight he woke up and saw the old ladies putting on white caps. "Here's off!" they shouted – and they flew out of the door! There was another white cap hanging on a hook. The boy put it on and shouted, "Here's off!" like the old ladies. At once he found himself flying after them.

They flew off to a rich man's mansion, down the chimney and into the cellar. There the old ladies tossed their caps aside. They started grabbing bottles of wine and cramming them into sacks. When they had finished, they flew back up the chimney, dragging the sacks behind them. But the boy did not have time to follow them, for the cellar door opened and the rich man strode in!

"You thief!" he yelled at the boy. "I'll whip you to death!"

Just in time, the boy managed to put on his magic cap. He whooshed up the chimney, he flew across the sky, and didn't stop until he reached his own house.

As soon as he was safely in his own bed, he hurled the flying cap right out of the window!

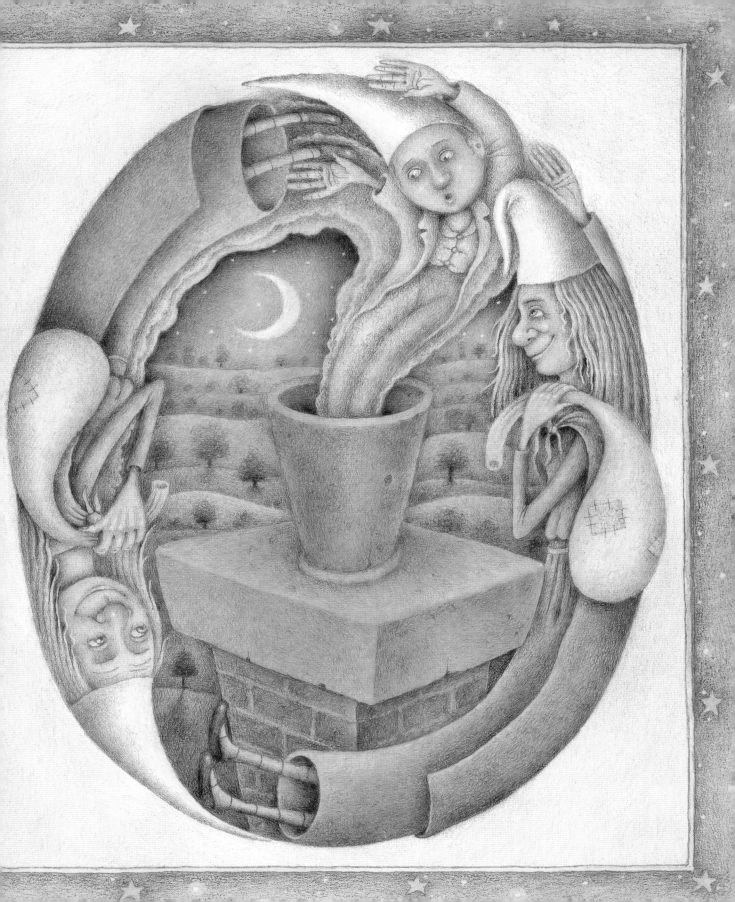

SECRET WORLDS

Scientists think that there are many other worlds out in space. Some people say there are magical worlds hidden here on Earth too.

Sky World

There is a secret world far above the skies of Africa and America. You can reach it by climbing a rope or a ladder hanging down from the clouds, or from a tree so tall that its highest branches are invisible.

In the Sky World, magic creatures live with the Sun, Moon and stars.

Fairyland

A magic world of fairies and dwarfs lies deep below the ground. The countryside of England, Ireland, Scotland and Wales is dotted with caves and rock doors leading into it.

Dragon Realms

At the seaside in China, Japan and Korea, the waves sometimes fall apart to reveal a golden path. It leads down to the underwater realm of the dragons! Here, fierce dragon kings and beautiful dragon princesses live in shimmering crystal palaces with silk furnishings. Their servants are fish, lobsters and crabs.

The dragon kings don't get many human visitors. If you ever find your way down there, they will be very pleased to see you. They might even give you a wonderful gift.

THE TURTLE AND THE DRAGON

A Japanese fisher-boy once saved a turtle from some other boys who were tormenting it. The next day, the grateful turtle swam up to the boy's boat. "Come with me," it cried. "I will take you to the palace of the Dragon King."

The turtle carried the boy on its back down through the waves. They came to a magnificent palace built of green and blue jewels, coral and pearls. It was surrounded by four gardens, one each for summer, autumn, winter and spring.

There, to the boy's astonishment, the turtle turned into a beautiful dragon princess! She fell in love with the fisher-boy. They got married and lived happily together in the Dragon Realms.

CELTIC OTHERWORLDS

The beautiful green lands of Wales and Ireland are often covered in thick mist. Are you brave enough to travel through them and over the swirling waters that lie beyond? Then you might come to Annwn, the Island of Joy, or the Land of Promise. The people in these Celtic Otherworlds feast every day, dance to enchanted music and drink the waters of magic springs. They are never ill, they never grow old and they live for ever.

Tir Na N'og lies off the west coast of Ireland, just beyond the setting sun. Sometimes lucky people are guided there by a beautiful princess, who carries them across the waves on horseback or in a glass-bottomed boat.

Avalon is the mysterious Isle of Apples or Glass. It lies on the far side of a forest lake in the west of England. Stories say that King Arthur was taken there to be healed by nine dark fairy queens, after he was wounded in his last battle.

LOOK FOR MAGIC!

A lot of people don't believe in magic.

Most grown-ups will tell you that science can explain

even the strangest things. They will say that "luck"

just happens by chance, that shape-changing and vanishing

are just tricks of the light, that nobody can fly or become invisible.

But these grown-ups may be wrong.

Maybe the world is full of strange forces.

Maybe their roots lie hidden deep in the earth and beyond the stars.

You can find signs of magic everywhere.

★

When you see a strange cloud formation, could it be

the walls and turrets of a magic world in the sky?

★

When you find that you can't stop dancing,

could the music be bewitched?

★

Has anything impossible happened to you?

★

Have you ever been bewitched

by a spell?

DO YOU BELIEVE IN MAGIC?

★ 45 ★

About the Stories

Stories about magic are told in every country of the world. No matter where they come from, they share similar themes of enchantment.

STONE-RIBS (p.13, *Native American*)
This story comes from the North-west coast of the United States and from Canada. The Native American people of this area have several heroes with supernatural powers.

RAINING JEWELS (p.16, *India*)
Here magic is linked to astronomy, because the spell only works once a year when the heavenly bodies are in the correct position.

THE WITCH'S SPELL (p.20, *England*)
This tale from the North Country was originally sung as a ballad.

THE SAUSAGE WISH (p.26, *Ireland*)
The idea of a wish being wasted or going wrong is also known as far away as China.

CERIDWEN'S CAULDRON (p.33, *Wales*)
This story is an ancient Celtic myth. However, Taliesin was a real Welsh poet who lived in the 6th century AD and worked in the court of King Maelgwn.

THE FLYING CAP (p.36, *Ireland, Scotland*)
Some versions of this tale have a strong historical setting and take the boy to 17th-century London. The two old women are probably witches.

THE TURTLE AND THE DRAGON (p.40, *Japan*)
The boy eventually becomes homesick and returns home to find that 300 years have passed. Similar stories about the undersea world of the Dragon Kings are common in China and Korea.